The World of MOTHER GOOSE

Illustrated by
GILES GREENFIELD

RP|KIDS
PHILADELPHIA · LONDON

Books published by Running Press are available at special discounts for bulk purchases in the
United States by corporations, institutions, and other organizations. For more information, please contact
the Special Markets Department at the Perseus Books Group, 2300 Chestnut Street, Suite 200,
Philadelphia, PA 19103, or call (800) 810-4145, ext. 5000,
or e-mail special.markets@perseusbooks.com.

9 8 7 6 5 4 3 2
Digit on the right indicates the number of this printing

Library of Congress Control Number: 2006938054

ISBN 978-0-7624-2312-5

Typography: Berkeley, Broken 15, Funny Bone, Metallophile
Perpetua, Stereopticon, and Voluta Script

Published by Running Press Kids
An Imprint of Running Press Book Publishers
A Member of the Perseus Books Group
2300 Chestnut Street
Philadelphia, PA 19103–4371

Visit us on the web!
www.runningpress.com/kids

TABLE OF CONTENTS

~ Classic Rhymes ~

CACKLE, CACKLE, MOTHER GOOSE

Cackle, cackle, Mother Goose,
Have you any feathers loose?
Truly have I, pretty fellow,
Half enough to fill a pillow.
Here are quills, take one or two,
And down to make a bed for you.

HUSH LITTLE BABY

Hush, little baby, don't say a word,
  Mama's going to buy you a mockingbird.

And if that mockingbird don't sing,
  Mama's going to buy you a diamond ring.

And if that diamond ring turns brass,
  Mama's going to buy you a looking glass.

And if that looking glass gets broke,
  Mama's going to buy you a billy goat.

And if that billy goat won't pull,
  Mama's going to buy you a cart and bull.

And if that cart and bull turn over,
  Mama's going to buy you a dog named Rover.

And if that dog named Rover won't bark,
  Mama's going to buy you a horse and cart.

And if that horse and cart fall down,
  You'll still be the sweetest little baby in town.

JACK

Jack be nimble, Jack be quick,
Jack jump over the candle-stick.

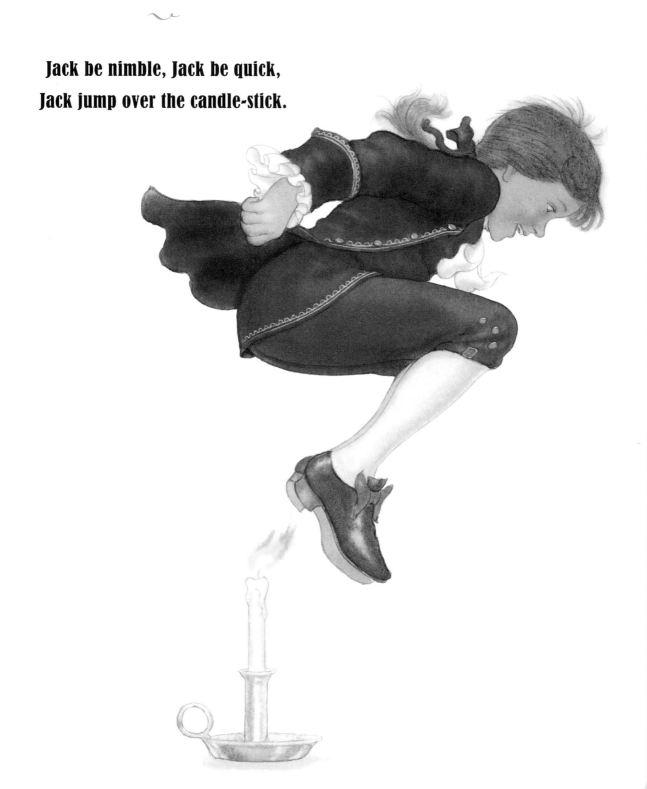

Ring A Ring
O' Roses

Ring a ring o' roses,

A pocketful of posies.

Tisha! Tisha!

We all fall down.

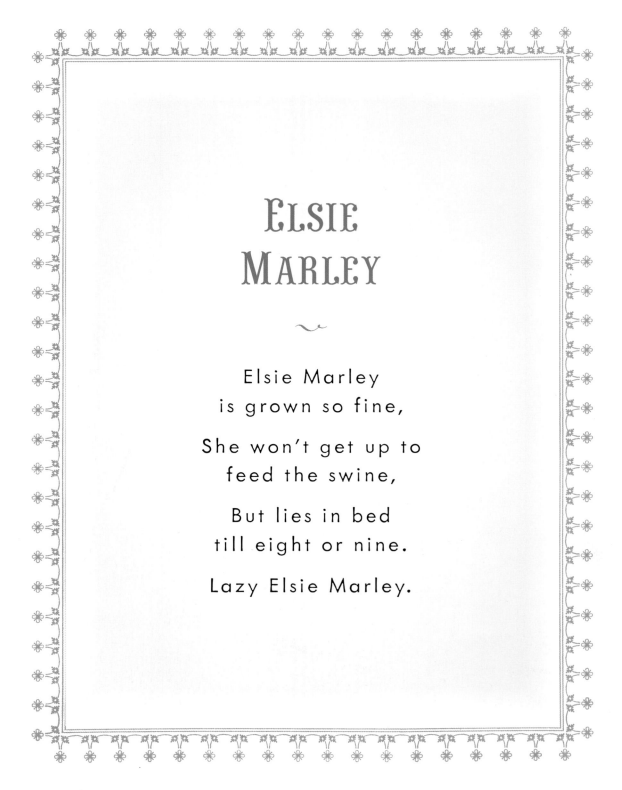

Elsie Marley

Elsie Marley
is grown so fine,

She won't get up to
feed the swine,

But lies in bed
till eight or nine.

Lazy Elsie Marley.

Jack and Jill

Jack and Jill went up the hill,
To fetch a pail of water;
Jack fell down, and broke his crown,
And Jill came tumbling after.

When up Jack got and off did trot,
As fast as he could caper,
To old Dame Dob, who patched his nob
With vinegar and brown paper.

DANCE TO YOUR DADDIE

~

Dance to your daddie,

My bonnie laddie;

Dance to your daddie,
my bonnie lamb;

You shall get a fishy,

On a little dishy;

You shall get a fishy,
when the boat comes home

LONDON BRIDGE

London Bridge is broken down,
Dance over my Lady Lee;
London Bridge is broken down,
With a gay lady.

How shall we build it up again?
Dance over my Lady Lee;
How shall we build it up again?
With a gay lady.

Build it up with silver and gold,
Dance over my Lady Lee;
Build it up with silver and gold,
With a gay lady.

Silver and gold will be stole away,
Dance over my Lady Lee;
Silver and gold will be stole away,
With a gay lady.

Build it up with iron and steel,
Dance over my Lady Lee;
Build it up with iron and steel,
With a gay lady.

Iron and steel will bend and bow
Dance over my Lady Lee;
Iron and steel will bend and bow
With a gay lady.

Build it up with wood and clay,
Dance over my Lady Lee;
Build it up with wood and clay,
With a gay lady.

Wood and clay will wash away,
Dance over my Lady Lee;
Wood and clay will wash away,
With a gay lady.

Build it up with stone so strong,
Dance over my Lady Lee;
Huzza! 'twill last for ages long,
With a gay lady.

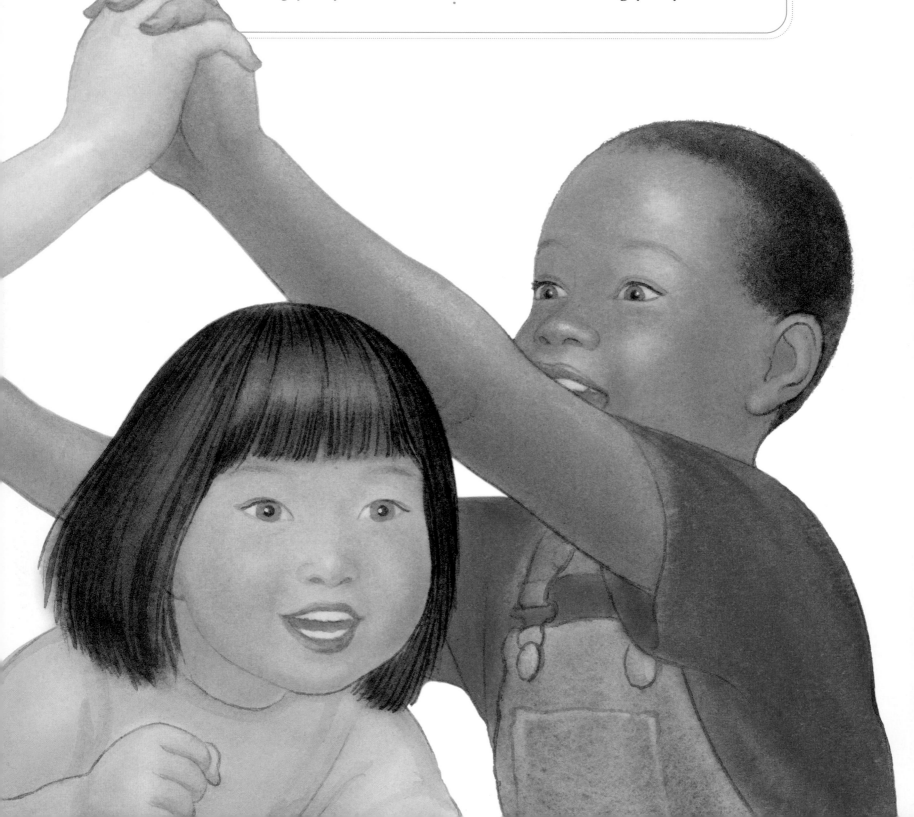

HIP-A-DI-HOP

Hip-a-di-hop to the barber shop
To buy a stick of candy,
One for me, and one for you,
And one for uncle Sandy.

Pop Goes The Weasel

Half a pound of tuppenny rice,
Half a pound of treacle.
That's the way the money goes,
Pop! goes the weasel.
Up and down the City road,
In and out the Eagle,
That's the way the money goes,
Pop! goes the weasel.

HUMPTY DUMPTY

Humpty Dumpty sat on a wall,

Humpty Dumpty had a great fall;

All the King's horses,
and all the King's men

Cannot put Humpty Dumpty
together again.

THE CROOKED SIXPENCE

There was a crooked man,
and he went a crooked mile,

He found a crooked sixpence
beside a crooked stile;

He bought a crooked cat,
which caught a crooked mouse,

And they all lived together
in a little crooked house.

JACK SPRAT

Jack Sprat
Could eat no fat,
His wife could eat no lean;
And so,
Betwixt them both,
They licked the platter clean.

I HAD A
LITTLE NUT TREE

I had a little nut tree,

Nothing would it bear,

But a silver nutmeg,

And a golden pear.

The King of Spain's daughter

Came to visit me,

And all for the sake

Of my little nut tree.

I skipped over water,

I danced over sea,

And all the birds in the air,

Couldn't catch me.

Cinderella

Cinderella, dressed in yellow
Went upstairs to kiss a fella
Made a mistake
And kissed a snake
How many doctors
Did it take?

THE BUNCH
OF BLUE RIBBONS

❧

Oh, dear,
what can the matter be?

Oh, dear,
what can the matter be?

Oh, dear,
what can the matter be?

Johnny's so long
at the fair.

❧

He promised
he'd buy me a bunch
of blue ribbons,

He promised
he'd buy me a bunch
of blue ribbons,

He promised
he'd buy me a bunch
of blue ribbons,

To tie up
my bonny brown hair.

The Ragman
and the Bagman

A ragman and a bagman came to a farmer's barn.

Said the ragman to the bagman,

"I'll do ye nae harm."

There are forty verses to my song,

And this is the first one just gone along.

A ragman and a bagman came to a farmer's barn.

Said the ragman to the bagman,

"I'll do ye nae harm."

There are forty verses to my song,

And this is the second one just gone along.

THE
LITTLE MOUSE

I have seen you, little mouse,

Running all about the house,

Through the hole your little eye

In the wainscot peeping sly,

Hoping soon some crumbs

    to steal,

To make quite a hearty meal.

Look before you venture out,

See if pussy is about.

If she's gone, you'll quickly run

To the larder for some fun;

Round about the dishes creep,

Taking into each a peep,

To choose the daintiest

    that's there,

Spoiling things you do not care.

Sing a Song of Sixpence

Sing a song of sixpence,
A pocket full of rye;
Four-and-twenty blackbirds
Baked in a pie!

When the pie was opened
The birds began to sing;
Was not that a dainty dish
To set before the king?

The king was in
his counting-house,

Counting out his money;

The queen was in the parlor,

Eating bread and honey.

The maid was in the garden,

Hanging out the clothes;

When down came a blackbird

And snapped off her nose.

LITTLE BO-PEEP

Little Bo-Peep has lost her sheep,
And can't tell where to find them;
Leave them alone, and they'll come home,
And bring their tails behind them.

Little Bo-Peep fell fast asleep,
And dreamt she heard them bleating;
But when she awoke, she found it a joke,
For still they all were fleeting.

Then up she took her little crook,
Determined for to find them;
She, found them indeed, but it made her heart bleed,
For they'd left all their tails behind 'em!

It happened one day, as Bo-peep did stray

Unto a meadow hard by—

There she espied their tails, side by side,

All hung on a tree to dry.

She heaved a sigh and wiped her eye,

And over the hillocks she raced;

And tried what she could, as a shepherdess should,

That each tail should be properly placed.

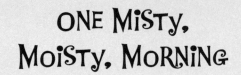

ONE MISTY, MOISTY, MORNING

One misty, moisty, morning,
When cloudy was the weather,
There I met an old man
All clothed in leather,
All clothed in leather,
With a cap under his chin.
How do you do?
And how do you do?
And how do you do again?

THE BLACK HEN

Hickety, pickety, my black hen,

She lays eggs for gentlemen;

Gentlemen come every day

To see what my black hen doth lay.

THIS LITTLE PIG

This little pig went to market;

This little pig stayed at home;

This little pig had roast beef;

This little pig had none;

This little pig said, **"WEE,**
WEE!
I can't find my way home."

COCK-A-DOODLE DOO

Cock-a-doodle-do!
My dame has lost her shoe,
My master's lost his fiddle-stick
And knows not what to do.

Cock-a-doodle-do!
What is my dame to do?
Till master finds his fiddle-stick,
She'll dance without her shoe.

OLD KING COLE

Old King Cole
Was a merry old soul,
And a merry old soul was he;

He called for his pipe,
And he called for his bowl,
And he called for
his fiddlers three!

And every fiddler, he had a fine fiddle,
And a very fine fiddle had he.
"Twee tweedle dee, tweedle dee,"
    went the fiddlers.

Oh, there's none so rare
As can compare
With King Cole and his fiddlers three.

MISS MUFFET

Little Miss Muffet

Sat on a tuffet,

Eating of curds and whey;

There came a big spider,

And sat down beside her,

And frightened Miss Muffet away.

MARY HAD
A LITTLE LAMB

Mary had a little lamb,
Little lamb, little lamb,
Mary had a little lamb,
Its fleece was white as snow.
And everywhere that Mary went,
Mary went, Mary went,
Everywhere that Mary went
The lamb was sure to go.

It followed her to school one day
School one day, school one day
It followed her to school one day
That was against the rule.
It made the children laugh and play,
Laugh and play, laugh and play,
It made the children laugh and play
To see a lamb at school.

And so the teacher turned it out,

Turned it out, turned it out,

And so the teacher turned it out,

But still it lingered near . . .

And waited patiently about,

Patiently about, patiently about,

And waited patiently about

Till Mary did appear.

"Why does the lamb
love Mary so?

Mary so? Mary so?

Why does the lamb
love Mary so?"

The eager children cry.

"Why, Mary loves the lamb,
you know.

The lamb, you know, the lamb,
you know!

Why, Mary loves the lamb,
you know."

The teacher did reply.

Widdy Dunn

There's a charming little widow,

And her name is on the door,

And that's where the children buy their chewing-gum.

She sells taffy for a penny,

And her name is on the door,

And there's music in the face of Widdy Dunn.

(Refrain)

Leena lanna, starry banana,

Happy day, boys, for every one!

Little buttercup,

Put your shutters up,

For there's music in the face of Widdy Dunn.

The cat and the Fiddle

Hey, diddle, diddle!

The cat and the fiddle,

The cow jumped over the moon;

The little dog laughed

To see such sport,

And the dish
ran away with the spoon.

Simple Simon

Simple Simon met a pieman,

    Going to the fair;

Says Simple Simon to the pieman,

    "Let me taste your ware."

    Says the pieman to Simple Simon,

        "Show me first your penny,"

    Says Simple Simon to the pieman,

        "Indeed, I have not any."

Simple Simon went a-fishing

    For to catch a whale;

All the water he could find

    Was in his mother's pail!

    Simple Simon went to look

        If plums grew on a thistle;

    He pricked his fingers very much,

        Which made poor Simon whistle.

He went to catch a dicky bird,

And thought he could not fail,

Because he had a little salt,

To put upon its tail.

He went for water with a sieve,

But soon it ran all through;

And now poor Simple Simon

Bids you all adieu.

LITTLE BOY BLUE

Little Boy Blue, come, blow your horn!

The sheep's in the meadow, the cow's in the corn.

Where's the little boy that looks after the sheep?

Under the haystack, fast asleep!

TOM, TOM, THE PIPER'S SON

Tom, Tom, the piper's son,
Stole a pig, and away he run,
The pig was eat,
And Tom was beat,
And Tom ran crying down the street

YANKEE DOODLE

Yankee Doodle came to town,
A-ridin' on a pony;
He stuck a feather in his hat
And called it macaroni.

Yankee Doodle keep it up,
Yankee Doodle Dandy;
Mind the music and the steps
And with the girls be handy.

Father and I went down to camp,
Along with Cap'n Goodwin;
The men and boys all stood around
As thick as hasty puddin'.

Yankee Doodle keep it up,
Yankee Doodle Dandy;
Mind the music and the steps
And with the girls be handy.

Cock-Crow

Cocks crow in the morn
To tell us to rise,
And he who lies late
Will never be wise;
For early to bed
And early to rise,
Is the way to be healthy
And wealthy and wise.

Anna Maria

Anna Maria
she sat on the fire.

The fire was too hot,
she sat on the pot.

The pot was too round,
she sat on the ground.

The ground was too flat,
she sat on the cat.

The cat ran away
with Maria on her back.

SKIP, ANGELINA

Skip, Angelina, do go home,
do go home,

Skip, Angelina, do go home,

To get your weddin' supper.

You better not wait till ten o'clock,
ten o'clock,

You better not wait till ten o'clock,

To get your weddin' supper.

Skip all around the cherry tree,
cherry tree,

Skip all around the cherry tree,

And get your weddin' supper.

Walk, Angelina, you go home,
you go home,

Ten o'clock will be too late,

To get your weddin' supper.

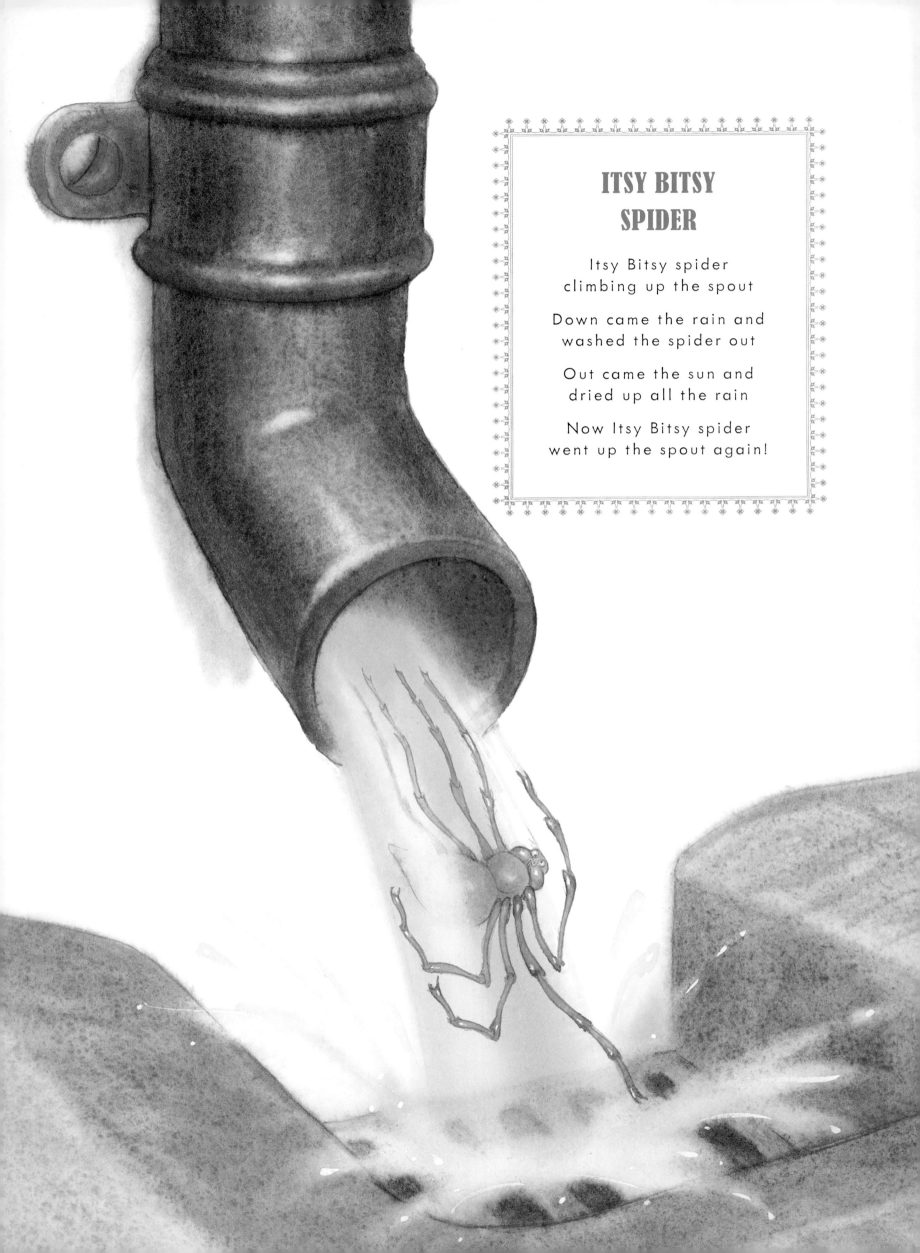

ITSY BITSY SPIDER

Itsy Bitsy spider
climbing up the spout

Down came the rain and
washed the spider out

Out came the sun and
dried up all the rain

Now Itsy Bitsy spider
went up the spout again!

TO MARKET

To market, to market,
  to buy a fat pig,

Home again, home again,
  jiggety jig.

To market, to market,
  to buy a fat hog,

Home again, home again,
  jiggety jog.

To market, to market,
  to buy a plum bun,

Home again, home again,
  market is done.

Baa, Baa, Black Sheep

Baa, baa, black sheep,
Have you any wool?
Yes, marry, have I,
Three bags full;

One for my master,
One for my dame,
But none for the little boy
Who cries in the lane.